How Do I Love You?

¿Cómo te Amo?

How Do I Love You?

¿Cómo te Amo?

P. K. Hallinan

ideals children's books.
Nashville, Tennessee

This Book Is for
Este libro es para

_____

From
De

_____

ISBN-13: 978-0-8249-5471-0

ISBN-10: 0-8249-5471-8

Published by Ideals Children's Books

An imprint of Ideals Publications

A Guideposts Company

535 Metroplex Drive, Suite 250

Nashville, Tennessee 37211

www.idealsbooks.com

Color separations by Precision Color Graphics

Franklin, Wisconsin

Printed and bound in Mexico by RR Donnelley

Text translated by Aide Urbano

Library of Congress CIP data on file

Cover design by Marisa Calvin

Book design by Jenny Eber Hancock

5 7 9 10 8 6 4

To Parents and Teachers:

How Do I Love You?, ¿Cómo te Amo?, is one of a series of bilingual books specially created by Ideals Children's Books to help children and their parents learn to read both Spanish and English.

Whether the child's native language is English or Spanish, he or she will be able to compare the text and, thus, learn to read both English and Spanish.

Also included at the end of the story are several common words listed in both English and Spanish that the child may review. These include both nouns, with their gender in Spanish, and verbs. In the case of the verbs, the Spanish verbs have the endings that indicate their use in the story.

Parents and teachers will want to use this book as a beginning reader for children who speak either English or Spanish.

A los Padres y los Maestros:

How Do I Love You?, ¿Cómo te Amo?, es parte de una serie de libros bilingüe hecho especialmente por Ideals Children's Books para ayudar a los niños y a sus padres a aprender como leer en Español e Inglés.

Cualquiera que sea el idioma nativo, el Inglés o el Español, el niño podrá comparar lo escrito y entonces aprenderá como leer en Inglés y en Español.

Al final de la historia hay una lista de vocabulario con palabras comunes en Inglés y en Español. La lista tiene ambos sustantivos, con el género y verbos en Español con los fines que indican el uso en la historia.

Los padres y los maestros desearán usar este libro como nivel inicial de lectura para niños que hablan Inglés o Español.

How do I love you?

Let me count the ways.

I love you on your very best . . .

¿Cómo te Amo?

Déjame contar las maneras.

Te amo por lo mejor . . .

and very worst of days.

y por lo peor de los días.

I love to see you laughing
And dancing in the rain.

Amo verte reír
y bailar en la lluvia.

And even when you lose your shoes,

I love you just the same.

Y aún cuando pierdes tus zapatos,

te amo igual.

I love to hear you singing.

Amo escucharte cantar.

I love to see you smile.

Amo ver tu sonrisa.

I love the way you take each day
In your own unhurried style.

Amo la manera en que pasas cada día
en tu propio estilo sin prisa.

I'm happy when you're happy,

Soy felíz cuando tú eres felíz,

And I'm sorry when you're sad.

Y lo siento cuando estás triste.

And even though it may not show,
I love you when you're mad.

Y aúnque no lo demuestre,
te amo cúando te enojas.

How do I love you?

Well, now, let me see . . .

I love the way you act so brave

When you fall and hurt your knee.

¿Cómo te Amo?

Bien, ahora déjame ver . . .

Amo la manera tan valiente en que actúas

cuando te caes y lastimas tu rodilla.

I love to watch you sleeping,
Tucked away in pleasant dreams.

Amo observarte dormido,
oculto en tus sueños agradables.

I love to hear you whisper
All your giant plans and schemes.

Amo escucharte susurrar
todos tus planes y proyectos gigantes.

I love the way you wear your pants
With the front part in the back,

Amo la manera como usas tus pantalones
con la parte de atrás para adelante,

And the way you
walk around sometimes
With your head inside a sack.

Y la manera en que caminas
algunas veces con tu cabeza dentro
de una bolsa de papel.

I love to see you deep in thought.

Amo verte cuando estás muy pensativo.

I love to watch you play.

Amo observarte jugar.

And though I'm sure
you'll never know,
I love you more each day.

Y casi estoy seguro
que nunca lo sabrás,
te amo cada día más.

How do I love you?
It's impossible to say.

For if I had a million days
And time enough for all the praise,
I couldn't tell you all the ways . . .

¿Cómo te amo?
es imposible decirlo.

Pero si tuviera un millón de días y el
tiempo suficiente para todos los elogios,
no podría decirte todas las maneras . . .

I love you.

Te amo.

Vocabulary words used in
How Do I Love You?
¿Cómo te Amo?

English	Spanish	English	Spanish
How	Cómo	shoes	zapatos
love	amo	singing	cantar
you	tu	hear	escucharte
count	contar	smile	sonrisa
ways	maneras	style	estilo
best	mejor	happy	felíz
worst	lo peor	sorry	siento
days	los días	sad	triste
see	verte	mad	enojado
laughing	reír	well	bien
dancing	bailar	now	ahora
the rain	la lluvia	let me	déjame
lose	pierdes	act	actúas
when	cuando	brave	valiente

English	Spanish
fall	caes
hurt	lastimas
knee	rodilla
sleeping	dormido
whisper	susurrar
giant	gigantes
pants	pantalones
head	cabeza
sack	una bolsa
thought	pensativo
watch	observarte
play	jugar
sure	seguro
more	más
each	cada
praise	los elogios
for	para
tell	decirte
impossible	imposible